THE BOOK OF THE HOWLAT

❖

To Daisy,

JAMES
ROBERTSON

THE BOOK OF THE HOWLAT

Illustrated by
KATE LEIPER

James Robertson   BC   *Kate Leiper*

It was a fine May morning, and Nature was smiling on everything in the world. The air was fresh, the fields were green, flowers were blooming, deer were grazing. A broad river flowed through a forest of tall trees, and as it went by them the trees bowed their branches to the water. Birds flitted from branch to branch, all singing happily. All, that is, except one.

Under the shade of a holly tree, one very miserable bird was cowering: a little owl, whose name was the Howlat. He was gazing into the water and groaning at his own reflection.

'Oh, why am I so ugly?' the Howlat wept. 'Why are my feathers so dowdy and fluffy, and my beak bent like an old hook? It must be because I'm an owl. It's not fair. I don't like sunlight — it hurts my stupid big eyes — so I hide all day and hope nobody sees me. The other birds hate me, I'm sure. If they do see me, they shriek at me and some try to peck me. And I don't blame them! It's not their fault I'm so horrible! It's Nature's fault for making me an owl.'

How the Howlat howled! But suddenly he had an idea. 'I know! The loveliest, most glamorous bird I've ever seen is the Peacock, who lives in the grounds of the castle. He must be one of Nature's favourites. I'll go and beg him to put in a good word for me, and ask Nature to change me. I don't want to be an owl.'

So the Howlat set off, keeping in the shadows as much as he could, until he found the Peacock, who was strutting up and down in the castle garden.

'I'm sorry to bother you,' the Howlat began, 'but I need your help.'

The Peacock spread his tail feathers and seemed to look at the Howlat with a hundred eyes.

'How can *I* help *you*?' he said.

'You can see for yourself what a foul little beast I am,' the Howlat moaned. 'As for my screeching voice — well, I'm sorry to inflict it on you even for a minute. Imagine if you had to live with it! It's not fair, and I don't deserve my fate. So would you kindly ask Nature, who has treated you so well, to make me beautiful too?'

'That may not be a good idea,' the Peacock replied. 'Nature doesn't usually make mistakes – although, I admit, you do look like one. I'll tell you what I'll do. I will call a council of all the fish-eating and seed-gathering birds, and the scavengers too, and see what *they* think.'

Then the Peacock summoned the Parrot and said, 'Where do we start?' And the Parrot said, 'Where do we start? Where do we start?', which was no help at all.

So the Peacock called the Wood Pigeon, who could write a little, and dictated the words of an invitation. The Wood Pigeon wrote it out many times, and as fast as she wrote (and she was fast, but she was also rather messy) the Swallows whisked the invitations away and delivered them far and wide.

Soon, birds were flying in from all directions:
a line of Cranes, with their bright red faces;
Swans, with their pure white breasts; Magpies,
Partridges, Plovers, Seagulls and Crows – all in
their different shades of black, white and grey.
The Woodpecker came, in his brightest outfit,
and even the Heron arrived, a little scruffy, and
stalked around not looking at anyone, as if he
didn't really mean to be there.

There was a gaggle of Geese, very full of themselves, and behind them the Raven, with his rough voice and bad manners. The Cockerel turned up, glancing this way and that, hoping to lead the choir if there was any singing. And the Curlew was made Secretary, because with her long beak she could write more neatly than the Wood Pigeon.

The Peacock welcomed them all, and asked the Howlat to address them.

'You can all see,' the Howlat said, 'how foul I am, just because I am an owl. It's not fair, when all I want is to be as handsome as the best of you. That's not too much to ask, is it? Nature has obviously made a mistake.'

But the council of birds, when they put their heads together, were not so sure about that. Some thought Nature really might have made a mistake; others thought it impossible. Some said, 'Moreover...' while others said, 'Besides...'. They felt sorry for the Howlat, but they could not decide what to do.

'We will have to consult more widely,' the Peacock announced. 'We will have to ask the *other* birds what they think.'

Not everybody was happy with this suggestion. The *other* birds were the birds of prey, who could be rather fierce. But they were also supposed to be very wise.

So the Curlew (helped, after a fashion, by the Wood Pigeon) wrote more letters, to the Eagle and the other birds of prey, and once again the Swallows delivered them as fast as they were written.

Then the birds of prey flew across the sea and over the mountains and forest to a green meadow by the river.

As well as the imperious Eagle, there were soaring Sea Eagles, gallant Goshawks, fierce Falcons, speedy Sparrow Hawks, bold Buzzards and magnificent Merlins. Even Robin Redbreast and the tiny Wren joined the great parade, hopping about cheekily among the big birds' legs.

A magnificent pavilion had been built, hung with silk tapestries, and with long tables set up, covered in gold cloth and spotless white linen. When all the birds had taken their places, the Peacock thanked them for coming and said, 'Let the feast begin.'

And what a feast there was! The Bittern was the cook, and the Gannets were the waiters, and wonderful dishes were served with savoury sauces. While they all ate, in came the minstrels — the Thrush, the Blackbird, the Lark and the Nightingale, with a chorus of Starlings. They sang songs giving thanks for the fruit, fish, grain and meat that Nature had provided.

After the minstrels, in came the Jay, who was
a juggler and conjurer. He juggled with gold-
rimmed goblets and made silver spoons vanish,
then reappear in other places! And he put a spell
on the whole company so that they believed it
was the dead of night, which gave them a fright
— although they laughed about it afterwards.

Next to do a turn was the Rook, a
Highland bard with a wicked laugh. 'Fill me with
food,' he squawked, 'or I'll make a rude rhyme
about you. Quench my thirst, or I'll spread stories
about you.' The Raven protested at these threats,
but the Rook made such a fool of him that he
blushed to the tips of his feathers and hid away in
a corner.

But then the Lapwing and the Cuckoo rushed
at the Rook together, covering
him in such a cloud of dirt that
he had to go outside for a wash.
That put an end to *his* act.
Everybody laughed so hard that
they almost forgot what they had
come for.

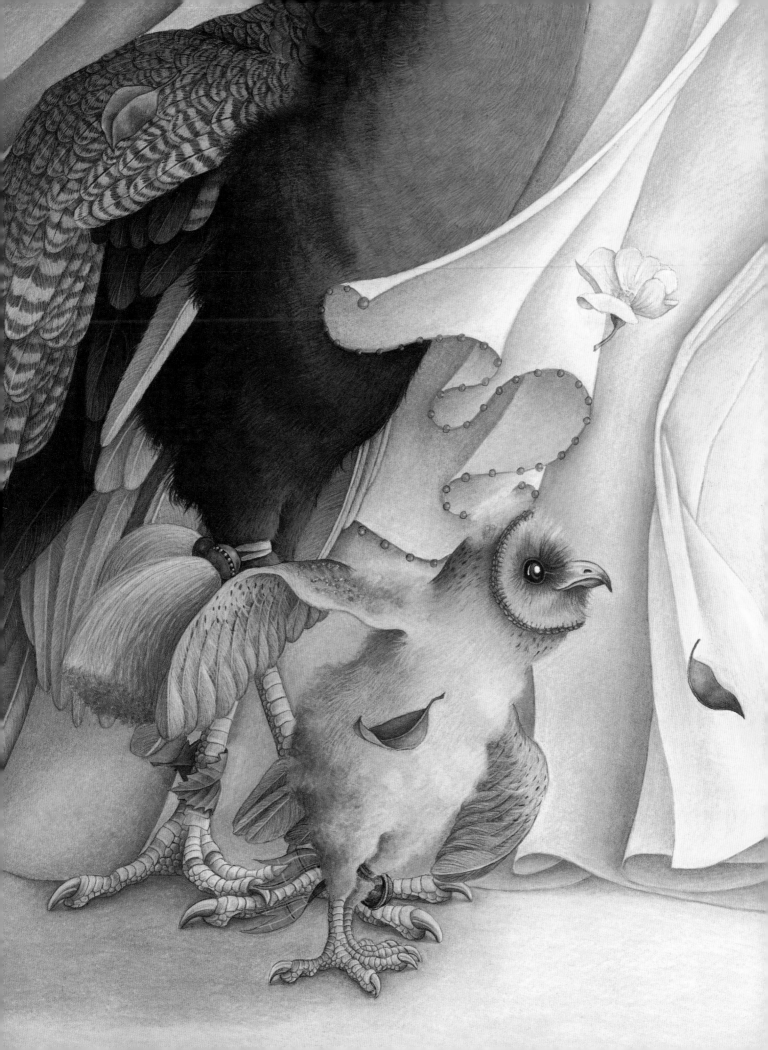

So the Peacock called the meeting to order. The Howlat made his appeal to the Eagle and the other birds of prey. 'I just want you to ask Nature to make me beautiful, like you,' he cried. 'You're so proud and strong – please have pity on poor little me!'

The birds of prey chewed their talons and looked down their beaks at the Howlat, but they did feel pity for him. They voted to put his request to Nature.

As soon as the vote had been taken, there was a shimmering in the air and the birds knew that Nature had come among them. 'No need to say a word,' Nature said. 'I will remake the Howlat, and this is how I will do it. Since you all feel so sorry for him, each of you shall take a feather from your own plumage and give it to the Howlat.'

So each bird gave a feather, and Nature made them into a cape and wrapped it round the Howlat. The Howlat inspected his new clothes. *How handsome I am!* he thought, *How shiny and posh my new plumage is! There's not a bird that can match me from Orkney to Berwick, from Aberdeen to Alloway!*

'Who's the prettiest now, Peacock?' the Howlat boasted. 'Eagle, what's it like to look so dull?' He was so haughty and conceited that he could not bear any of the other birds to come close. 'Keep back, you rascals!' he shrieked. 'I feel sick just looking at you.'

The other birds were very annoyed with this behaviour. They gathered together and raised a great complaint about the result of Nature's meddling.

'I only did what you asked,' Nature told them, 'but in fact what you asked was not possible. Even Nature cannot change nature.'

Then Nature turned to the Howlat. 'I raised you up, but now I shall bring you down. An owl you were, and an owl you shall be once more. Each bird will take back its feather, and leave you in your own clothes.'

So this was done, and Nature departed, and all the birds flew home to their nests. The Howlat was left alone as night fell and the moon rose.

But the Howlat had changed! The dowdy, fluffy thing he had been was no more. In its place was a bigger, stronger bird, with a full coat of feathers! He himself was a bird of prey. In the moonlight he looked quite magnificent, and wise too!

'Oh, oh, I see now!' the Howlat cried, and his voice carried far through the trees. 'I am not a bird of the daylight. I am a bird of the night. I wanted to be something I could not be, when what I had to do was be patient, until I grew into myself. I have learned a good lesson. To be truly happy, you have to be true to your own nature.'

And the Howlat flew
into the night. And that,
of course, is where he belongs.

THE BUKE OF THE HOWLAT

This story is taken from a poem, a beast fable, written in Older Scots in the 1440s by Richard Holland. Like *Animal Farm*, fables such as this are a means of looking at complex human issues. The poem is set at and around Darnaway Castle in Moray and is dedicated to the Countess of Moray, Elizabeth Dunbar, and her husband, Archibald Douglas. At this period the Black Douglas family was a major power in Scotland and the centre of Holland's poem (omitted here) is a display of heraldry linking the Douglas family with the major powers of Europe. The heart on the Douglas arms celebrates 'Good Sir James' taking the heart of Robert the Bruce on crusade. Like the owl in the poem, however, the family are subject to the levelling of death, but their reputation lives on.

In the 1450s the Douglas family fell out of favour and Holland was exiled. His poem however survived, was one of the first printed in Scotland and was known to many of the greatest Older Scots poets.

The text of Holland's poem can be found in Richard Holland, *The Buke of the Howlat*, ed. R. Hanna, Scottish Text Society 5.12 (Edinburgh: Scottish Text Society, 2014).

NICOLA ROYAN

Acknowledgements

When a new edition of *The Buke of the Howlat* was published by the Scottish Text Society, it was the ideal opportunity to bring the poem and its narrative to a wider audience, first through its launch at Darnaway Castle and then through this publication. I see it as a story of the challenges facing the young Howlat on that journey from childhood to adolescence, a story that through an inspired illustrator and inspiring author can now be shared in English and in Scots by a new generation of children, their parents and grandparents. Crucially, it is a story set in Moray, that microcosm of the best of Scotland.

In transforming *The Buke of the Howlat* for younger audiences I am indebted to: Nicola Royan and Ralph Hanna of the Scottish Text Society for opening my eyes to this poetic gem; Cameron Taylor for recognising the potential of a children's edition; Sheila Campbell, Moray Council Libraries, for identifying the perfect illustrator in Kate Leiper from Moray and directing me to Hugh Andrew; Hugh Andrew and Birlinn for finding the perfect partner writer in James Robertson and for being the ideal publisher; my wife, Jean, who has been supportive in seeing this story move from Darnaway Forest to printed page; and Lord and Lady Moray for making Darnaway Castle available for launches of *The Buke of the Howlat*.

JIM ROYAN

First published in 2016
by BC Books, an imprint of Birlinn Limited
West Newington House, 10 Newington Road,
Edinburgh EH9 1QS

www.bcbooksforkids.co.uk

ISBN 978 1 78027 375 4

British Library Cataloguing-in-Publication Data
A catalogue record for this book is available from
the British Library

*For Yasmin, with lots
of love KL*

The publishers acknowledge investment from Creative Scotland towards the publication of this
book and would like to thank Jim Royan, without whose unstinting enthusiasm and support this project
could not have been undertaken.

Design and art direction by James Hutcheson • Printed and bound by Livonia, Latvia